John Grisham lives with his family in Virginia and Mississippi. His novels are *A Time to Kill*, *The Firm*, *The Pelican Brief*, *The Client*, *The Chamber*, *The Runaway Jury*, *The Partner* and *The Street Lawyer*.

BY THE SAME AUTHOR